Disney

Bambi

Ladybird

One spring morning, just as the sun was rising, animals and birds hopped, scurried and fluttered to a quiet thicket in the middle of the forest. As they went, they spread the exciting news: "The new Prince is born! Come and see!"

The new Prince was a small, spotted fawn, the son of the noble stag who was the Great Prince of the Forest. All the animals and birds gathered round to admire the new baby as he slept by his mother's side.

"Congratulations," they said to Mother Deer.

"Thank you," she said, gently nuzzling her fawn.

"What will you call him?" asked a young rabbit named Thumper.

"Bambi," replied Mother Deer, and all the animals nodded.

It wasn't long before Bambi was ready to explore the forest with his mother. Each day they walked through the wood, and all the animals and birds greeted them.

"Good morning, Bambi! Good morning, young Prince!" chirped Mother Quail and her nine babies.

Bambi learned that the forest was a fascinating place, and that he had friends all around him.

Bambi soon made a special friend – Thumper the rabbit. Thumper showed him all the best places to play, and taught him how to hop over logs.

Thumper also taught Bambi to say his first word – *bird*. Bambi was so proud of himself that he said it over and over: "Bird, bird, bird!" he cried happily.

When Bambi saw a bright yellow butterfly fluttering through the air, he called, "Bird!"

"No," said Thumper, "that's a butterfly!"

"Butterfly!" repeated Bambi, as he leapt into a bed of white and yellow flowers.

"No, that's a flower!" laughed Thumper. He sniffed one. "It's pretty," he told Bambi.

"Flower," said Bambi, as he bent to sniff the flowers too. Suddenly a little black-and-white head popped up from under the flowers.

"Flower!" said Bambi again.

Thumper giggled. "That's not a flower, that's a skunk!" he said.

"That's all right," said the little skunk shyly. "He can call me Flower if he wants to!"

Bambi had made another friend.

One day Bambi's mother took him to a very special place – the meadow.

The meadow was wide and open, with no trees for protection, so they had to be very careful. Bambi's mother went ahead to make sure there was no danger, then she called Bambi to come to her.

Bambi loved the meadow. It was so much fun to run and leap across the open spaces, and the tall grass tickled his legs.

There were other deer in the meadow too, and one of them was a fawn just the same age as Bambi. She came up to Bambi and wagged her tail in friendship.

Bambi had never seen another fawn before. Overcome with shyness, he rushed back to his mother and tried to hide.

"It's all right, Bambi," his mother assured him. "That's Faline. She just wants to be friends with you. Go and say hello."

Timidly, Bambi went back to Faline. She giggled and began chasing him. Bambi couldn't resist chasing her in return. Soon the two fawns were laughing and skipping together, enjoying an exciting game of hide-and-seek in the rushes. Their mothers watched them happily.

All at once, Bambi and Faline heard the thunder of hoofbeats. They clambered up onto a rock and saw a large group of stags charging across the meadow. The herd bounded through the grass, leaping far and high as they ran.

Bambi followed the galloping stags, until they stopped suddenly. There in front of them was a very tall deer, with many-branched antlers. It was the Great Prince of the Forest. Everyone stood in awe of him. He walked towards Bambi looking proudly down at his son. Then the Great Prince walked regally into the woodland, and the rest of the deer began to charge again.

It was not long before the Great Prince returned. He had come to warn the animals that danger was nearby.

All the deer raced towards the trees. Faline's mother rushed to her daughter's side and they ran together to their forest home. Bambi could not find his own mother and started to panic. But there beside him was the Great Prince, pointing out the way to go. Bambi ran with him into the wood and was overjoyed to find his mother running with them too.

Back in the safety of the thicket, Bambi asked his mother what the danger had been.

"Man was in the forest," was all she replied. She was very glad that the hunters and their guns had gone – for now.

One morning when Bambi woke up, the world looked different. It was covered in a thick, sparkling, white blanket.

"That's snow, Bambi," his mother told him. "Winter has come."

Bambi walked out into the snow. It was crisp and cold, and his hooves sank into it and made holes where he stepped. Snow was full of surprises!

Bambi was having fun making hoofprints when he heard Thumper calling him. He looked up and saw Thumper sliding across the pond. Bambi was amazed!

"The water's stiff!" Thumper cried. "Come on, you can skate too!"

Bambi ran down and leapt onto the frozen pond, just as he'd seen Thumper do. But his hooves were too small to balance on the slippery surface, and he landed – *SPLAT!* – right on his tummy.

Thumper laughed and tried to help his friend glide across the ice. Soon Bambi was whizzing along.

"Whee!" cried Thumper. "This is fun!"

Winter was a happy time at first, but Bambi soon learned that it was a difficult time as well. No matter how raw and cold it was, the deer could not hide in their snug thicket. They had to spend all their time searching for food, which was growing scarce.

At last the hungry deer had nothing to eat but the bark on the trees. When Bambi could no longer reach for himself his mother tore off strips from higher up the tree and gave them to her son.

One day, when the air seemed a bit warmer, Bambi and his mother went to the meadow to look for food. There they found a little patch of green peeping through the snow.

"It's new spring grass," Bambi's mother said. "This means that winter will be over before too long."

The grass was more delicious than anything Bambi had ever tasted. He and his mother ate eagerly, trying to fill their empty stomachs.

Suddenly Bambi's mother looked up. Her ears twitched, and she sniffed the air. She sensed danger nearby.

"Go to the thicket," she told Bambi. "Quickly! Run!"

Bambi raced across the meadow. All at once he heard a loud *BANG!*

"Faster, Bambi!" called his mother, right behind him. "Run, and don't look back!"

The fear in her voice made Bambi frightened, too, and he ran even faster. Suddenly there was another *BANG*, louder than the first. Terror surged through him as he tore through the forest, desperate to reach home.

At last, in the shelter of the thicket, Bambi stopped. Breathless, he listened for his mother's hoofbeats behind him. But there was only silence.

"Mother!" he called. "Mother, where are you?"

There was no answer.

Bambi's heart thumped with panic as he looked around for his mother. "Mother, where are you?" he called again and again.

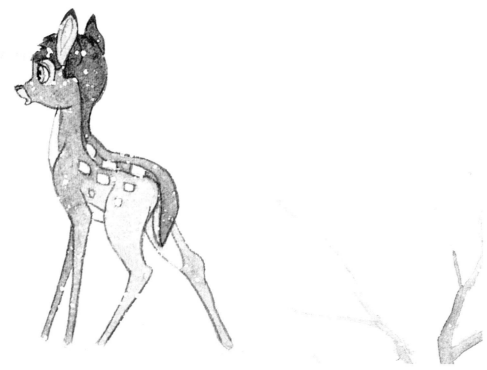

The Great Prince of the Forest came to Bambi's side.

"Your mother cannot be with you any longer," he said to Bambi.

Bambi began to cry, remembering the loud *BANGS*. Man's guns had taken his mother from him for ever.

"Come, my son," said the Great Prince. "You must be brave and learn to walk alone now."

Staying close to his father, Bambi walked silently through the forest. He knew he would miss his mother, and he would remember her always.

The long, harsh winter ended at last, and spring returned to the forest. Leaves appeared on the trees, green shoots poked through the ground and flowers bloomed.

All the young animals were eager to see one another again. Thumper the rabbit hopped up onto a log and began thumping with his big foot.

"Bambi!" he called. "It's Thumper. Remember me?"

Flower's stripy head popped up from a patch of daisies. He had had a long sleep over the winter, and now he was rested and full of energy.

"Hi there, fellows!" he called. Like Thumper, he had grown bigger and had a deeper voice.

Bambi greeted his old friends happily. The spots had faded from his coat, and on his head he proudly carried a brand-new set of antlers.

As the three friends strolled through the wood together, Flower noticed a pretty female skunk smiling shyly at him. Suddenly Flower felt happy and tingly all over.

"Uh-oh," said Thumper, watching Flower walk away with the other skunk. "Flower's twitterpated! Owl says it happens to everyone in springtime!"

"Well, it won't happen to me!" Bambi declared.

"Me, neither!" agreed Thumper. But a moment later a lovely young female rabbit hopped up and said hello to him. Thumper gazed at her with a rapturous expression, then settled down happily to listen as she sang to him.

"Twitterpated!" muttered Bambi to himself.

Bambi continued on his way alone. He came to a small pond and was just leaning down for a drink when he heard a soft voice say, "Hello, Bambi."

A beautiful young doe was standing beside him. "Don't you remember me?" she said. "I'm Faline."

Bambi suddenly felt foolish and awkward. He tried to back away, but his antlers got caught in a branch. Faline came closer and gently licked his face. Bambi winced, expecting to be annoyed, but he was surprised to discover he enjoyed it!

Bambi was so happy, he felt as if he were floating. Together, he and Faline walked through the forest towards the meadow where they had played as young fawns.

All at once a strong young stag burst through the bushes. "You're not going any further," he said to Bambi. "Faline is coming with me!" He pushed Bambi out of the way and tossed his antlers at Faline. The stag drove her deeper into the wood, away from the young Prince.

"Bambi!" she cried, frightened and confused.

Bambi had never been in a fight before, but he could not let this rough bully harm Faline. Lowering his head, he charged at the other stag with all his might.

The two stags locked antlers and tossed one another this way and that. The stranger was stronger and more experienced than Bambi, and with a powerful twist of his head, he flung Bambi to the ground.

But Bambi was determined not to be defeated, and he got up and charged again. His antlers crashed into the other stag's, and this time Bambi managed to throw him down.

Bambi waited for the other stag to get up and attack again. But the stranger limped away without a word. Bambi had won.

Faline rushed up and brushed her face against his neck. Then they walked on to the meadow, to begin their new life together.

The warm, sweet days of spring and summer passed quickly.

Early one autumn morning, a strange scent in the air woke Bambi. Careful not to disturb Faline as she slept beside him, he left the thicket to find out what it was.

Standing on a cliff high above the wood, Bambi saw smoke rising from a clearing. His father came up beside him. "Man has returned," he told Bambi. "Those are his campfires. We must go deep into the forest – quickly!"

Bambi hurried away to warn Faline.

But Faline was not where he had left her. When she had woken up and found Bambi gone, she had panicked and run off to look for him.

"Bambi!" she cried, as she darted through the trees. All at once the sound of gunfire rang out, and a pack of hunting dogs came tearing through the wood. Faline ran quickly, but they bounded after her, barking and nipping at her heels.

Terrified, Faline managed to climb onto a rocky ledge. "Bambi!" she cried desperately, as the snarling dogs leapt up at her.

Hearing her cries, Bambi sped towards Faline. He rushed at the pack of dogs, distracting them so that Faline could escape.

Bambi managed to fight the dogs off and make his own escape. But just when he thought he was safe, he heard a loud *BANG!*

A searing pain shot through Bambi's shoulder, and he fell to the ground.

As he lay there, Bambi could smell smoke drifting closer and closer. The flames from Man's campfires were spreading. He knew he should try to get up, but he was too weak.

"Get up, Bambi!" said a deep voice above him. It was his father, the Great Prince of the Forest. "The forest is on fire," he said. "You must get up!"

Slowly, painfully, Bambi struggled to his feet.

"We must go to the lake," said the Great Prince. "Come with me."

As Bambi followed his father, his strength returned. Together they sprang this way and that to find a safe path through the blaze.

At last they reached the lake. In the middle of the water was an island, where many animals had already found safety. Bambi and the Great Prince swam towards it.

Faline was waiting for them. She was so relieved and grateful to see that Bambi was alive!

Safe on the island, the forest creatures looked across the lake and watched the flames sweep through their homes. Though they were glad to have escaped with their lives, they all wondered the same thing – would there be anything to go back to when the fire died down?

They eventually returned to find that their homes had been destroyed. The forest had been badly damaged, but it had survived the fire. When spring came, green shoots sprang up once more, bringing new life from the ashes.

One warm morning, Owl was awakened by a family of rabbits thumping loudly beneath his tree.

"Wake up, friend Owl!" called Thumper and his four children.

"Oh, what now?" asked Owl sleepily. "What's going on around here?"

But the rabbits were too excited to stay and explain.

Owl, wondering what all the excitement was about, followed their path as they scampered through the forest.

They were soon joined by Flower and his family, squirrels, raccoons, and chipmunks, all going in the same direction. Overhead, birds darted through the branches, chattering loudly.

"What's going on?" Owl asked again.

"Haven't you heard?" said Flower. "It's happened!"

"Happened?" asked Owl.

"Yes," said Flower. "In the thicket!"

Still confused, Owl made his way to the thicket. As soon as he got there, he understood what all the fuss was about.

For there, surrounded by a crowd of admiring animals, was Faline. And snuggled close to her were two brand-new spotted fawns.

"Ahhh!" sighed the animals. "Look! Twins!"

"Prince Bambi must be awfully proud!" said Owl.

Bambi was indeed very proud. Standing on a nearby hilltop, he gazed down at Faline and their two fawns, and his heart swelled with joy. He knew that he would love and protect them, just as his own father had loved and protected him – and all the forest creatures.

For now he, Bambi, was the new Great Prince of the Forest, and he looked forward to the years ahead.